Contents

Chapter One   5

Chapter Two   16

Chapter Three   28

Chapter Four   45

Chapter Five   57

Chapter Six   68

Chapter Seven   82

Chapter Eight   93

Chapter Nine   110

Chapter Ten   125

Chapter Eleven   133

Chapter Twelve   143

CHAPTER ONE

"Faster, Ember! Faster!" Amara cried, her hands clinging to Ember's neck and her plaits flying out as he galloped around the meadow. His hooves pounded on the summer grass and the magical golden flames of his mane flicked over her hands, tickling but not hurting her.

Most of the time, Ember looked like a beautiful coal-black pony with a silky mane and tail, but now he was in his true magical shape – as an elemental horse – and Amara could feel the magic surging through him. Being a True Rider was the best thing ever!

Elemental horses only bonded with one person, someone who could help them control their magic and use it for good – their True Rider. Each elemental horse could control one of the four elements – earth, air, fire and water. Ember was a fire horse and could set things alight.

Stopping in the centre of the meadow, Ember reared up and as he landed, he transformed back into his pony form. Amara slid from his back. "I love you so much," she said, kissing his nose.

Ember nuzzled her face. *And I love you. Do you think we'll get to gallop like that on the beach when we're on holiday?*

Amara grinned. She loved that she could hear Ember's thoughts. "Definitely. Alex and Imogen said it was one of the best bits of the holiday last year."

Amara and her three best friends at Moonlight Stables – Kalini, Imogen and Alex – were about to go on holiday to Seaview Stables. Alex and Imogen had been the year before and had told Amara and Kalini how brilliant it was. There would be riding lessons in the morning and beach hacks and woodland rides in the afternoon. They would swim in the sea and hang out on the beach, and in the evenings they would have campfires. At the end of the week there would be a mini One Day Event – a riding competition where the riders took part in showjumping, cross country and dressage.

Imogen, Kalini and Alex were True Riders as well. Kalini's horse was a dapple-grey stallion called Thunder, a Wind Horse with power over storms. Imogen's was a pretty snow-white mare called Tide, a Water Horse. Alex's horse was a chunky chestnut with a flaxen mane and tail called Rose, an Earth Horse with power over plants.

Ember looked to where Thunder, Tide and Rose were grazing along with the other five elemental horses who lived at Moonlight Stables – Sandy, Sirocco, Forest, Sparks and Cloud. *We'll have to keep our magic secret while we're away,* he said.

Amara nodded. No one was allowed to know about the elemental horses unless they were a True Rider or a Legacy Rider – someone whose parent or grandparent had been a True Rider.

"Amara!" She glanced round. Kalini, Imogen and Alex were climbing over the meadow gate, headcollars in their hands and excited grins on their faces.

"It's holiday time!" shouted Alex. "Seaview Stables, here we come!"

"Midnight feasts. Swimming in the sea,"

said Imogen, pushing her glasses up her nose.

"Pony quizzes and riding every single day," added Kalini happily.

Amara grinned. "This is going to be the best holiday ever!" she declared.

They groomed their ponies while Jill Reed, the owner of the stables, got the horsebox out.

Jill had been a True Rider but her elemental horse, Shula, had died in an accident. Since then, Jill had devoted her life to helping elemental horses find their True Riders and to giving a home to any elemental horse who needed it. Amara didn't know the details of Shula's accident, but she knew it had something to do with Ivy Thornton, the owner of nearby Storm Stables. Ivy and Jill had once been friends but then Ivy had become a Night Rider – someone who used the elemental horses' power for selfish ends.

As they led the ponies across the yard to the horsebox, Amara had a thought. "One really good thing about going on holiday is that we won't have to see any of the Storm Stables riders for at least a week."

"Yay!" said Kalini.

The Storm Stables riders were horrible. Three of them – Zara, Daniela and Shannon – rode elemental horses and they hated the riders at Moonlight Stables. Zara and Daniela were cousins and they were both as mean as each other.

"I hope the other people on the holiday

are nice," said Imogen, leading Tide up the ramp of the horsebox. "We made some good friends last year, didn't we, Alex?"

He nodded. "Like Willow. She's the daughter of Sue who owns Seaview. She's brilliant fun."

"She likes playing pranks on people," said Imogen, her greeny-brown eyes sparkling behind her glasses. "So, beware!"

They helped Jill heave the ramp into place.

"How long will it take us to get there?" Kalini asked.

"About two hours," said Jill, pushing her chin-length blonde hair back from her face. Her skin was tanned from working outdoors all her life. "I'm looking forward to seeing Sue again. We grew up together and we're still good friends."

Just then, a car pulled up to the gate and a tall, slim girl with dark brown hair jumped out.

"Malia!" Amara called, waving. Malia kept her dressage pony, Goldie, at the stables.

Malia jogged up the driveway. "I thought I'd come and see you all before you go." Malia had wanted to come with them but she had a big three-day dressage event later that week and there was no way she could miss it. "Make sure you ring me and send me loads of photos!" she said.

"We will!" they chorused.

Amara, Alex, Imogen and Kalini travelled to Seaview in the living quarters of the horsebox. It seemed to take for ever to get there but at long last Jill turned up a long, straight drive that had a sign saying: *Seaview Stables.*

At the top of the drive there was a parking area, a farmhouse with an orchard and a large single storey log cabin to one side. Next to the farmhouse there was a yard with an old brick stable block and a large modern American-style barn with twenty more stables for the campers' horses. People were milling around, unloading ponies and carrying tack and grooming kits.

Amara smiled happily as she breathed in the salty air and heard the seagulls crying out overhead. This was it! Their holiday was about to start!

But just then she saw something that made her heart plummet. Across the parking lot

a slim girl with long, curly blonde hair was leading a striking chestnut pony down the ramp of a gleaming black horsebox with a lightning flash on its side. The blonde girl was followed by a tall girl with auburn hair leading a stocky bay pony with a glossy coat and thick black mane and tail.

"Zara and Daniela!" Amara said in dismay as she recognised the Storm Stables riders. "What are they doing here?"

CHAPTER TWO

"Oh no," Imogen gasped, following Amara's gaze. "Zara and Daniela are here too."

"Move!" snapped Zara, leading her horse, Scorch, straight towards a younger girl who had to jump quickly to one side to avoid being trampled.

"Where are our ponies' stables?" called Daniela, following Zara with Quake. "We need the best stables, you know. These are very valuable ponies." She shot a snooty look at a couple of small hairy ponies that were tied up to a trailer they were passing.

A thin woman in very smart riding clothes with her hair tied back in a bun and hairnet came marching out of the American barn.

Ivy Thornton. Amara felt a shiver run down her spine as she looked at the woman's hard face.

"This way, girls," Ivy said. "I've spoken to Sue and sorted out the two largest stables for you."

"I can't believe Zara and Daniela are here," groaned Alex. "They're going to ruin everything!"

"No, they won't," said Kalini, her hazel eyes flashing with determination. "We won't let them."

Imogen nodded. "There's no way they're

going to stop us having a good time."

Amara hoped she was right!

They unloaded the ponies and all their stuff. Jill introduced them to Sue, who owned Seaview, and they met Safiya, a young woman who worked for Sue. Safiya was going to be staying in the cabin with the campers each night.

Sue's ten-year-old daughter, Willow, showed Amara and the others which stables their ponies would be in. She was very friendly with a wide smile and curly red hair. Her cheeks had a smattering of freckles and her eyes were a pale green. Amara also noticed that her left arm was shorter than her right and she didn't have a left hand, but only having one hand didn't seem to hinder Willow at all.

After the ponies were settled in their stables, she helped them carry their saddles and bridles to the tack room and explained to them how the holiday would be organised.

"Mum and Saffy have split the riders into two troops depending on how experienced they are and how high they like jumping." She checked a list on the tack room wall. "Amara and Kalini, you're in the Blue Troop with me. That's the group for the slightly less experienced riders and riders who don't like jumping really high. We'll be

taught by Saffy. Alex and Imogen, you're in the Red Troop and will be taught by Mum. You'll get to do all the scary jumps on the cross-country course."

"Cool!" said Alex.

"We were in the Blue Troop last year," said Imogen. "It'll be awesome to get to jump the big jumps this year."

Kalini tucked her arm through Amara's. "I think I'll be happy in the Blue Troop."

Amara felt the same. She and Kalini were definitely less experienced than Imogen and Alex and it would be fun getting to know Willow better.

"The Blue Troop have the stables on the right-hand side of the barn and the Red Troop have the stables on the left," Willow carried on. "Every day there will be inspections and the troops will earn points depending on how clean their stables, tack and ponies are."

"You can also get points for being particularly kind or helpful," said Imogen.

"Or for doing really well in the riding lessons," Alex added.

"At the end of the week, the troop with the most points wins a prize," said Willow.

"Do you get to join in with every riding camp, all through the holidays?" Kalini asked her enviously.

"Yep!" Willow grinned. "Living here is brilliant!"

Zara and Daniela came into the barn. Their riding clothes were pristine and they always liked to mention how expensive they were. Zara was wearing turquoise and Daniela was in hot pink. "I can't believe we actually have to muck out our own ponies," Zara was saying to Daniela. "I mean, I thought there'd be grooms here. Like at Storm Stables."

"It's crazy," said Daniela. "I don't want to have to muck out on my holiday." She saw Willow. "Hey you," she called sharply. "You live here, don't you?"

"Yes, I'm Willow," said Willow, giving them a friendly smile. "Can I help you?"

"You can get our things from our horsebox now," said Daniela.

"But be careful," snapped Zara. "Our tack is very expensive."

Willow's mouth fell open.

"Get your own things!" Alex said hotly. "Just because Willow lives here doesn't mean she has to run round after you."

Willow put her hand on his arm. "It's OK." She turned to the older girls. "I think you've got the wrong idea," she said politely but firmly. "Everyone on holiday here must look after their own pony and sort their own things out. I'm happy to show you where to put your things but it's your own responsibility to look after them."

Zara and Daniela glared at her and stalked away.

Amara grinned at Kalini. Willow might be younger than them, but she was clearly more than capable of standing up for herself.

Once the adults had left, the riders went into the log cabin for an early lunch. There was a large kitchen with a huge table and a common room with a TV, comfy sofas and lots of horse books. Linking the two rooms was a corridor with bedrooms on both sides and four bathrooms. Willow explained to the others that although she would be doing all the riding activities with them, she would sleep in the farmhouse with her mum.

The campers piled their things up in the common room and then sat down at the kitchen table. It was laid with massive plates of sandwiches – tuna, ham, cheese, egg as well as big bowls of crisps, little tomatoes and pieces of cucumber.

While everyone tucked in, Sue talked to them all about the week ahead.

"I hope you're all going to have a great time here. There's going to be lots to do – riding lessons in the morning, hacks in the afternoon, chances to earn points for your troops and of course the Summer Camp One Day Event Showdown at the end."

Amara looked round the table at all her fellow campers. There was a mix of boys and girls and they all looked excited – all apart from Zara and Daniela, who were rolling their eyes at each other as if they found everything Sue was saying boring.

"There are just a few rules," Sue went on. "No one is to go into the barn before 7.30 a.m. or after 6.30 p.m., apart from at 9.00 p.m. when we'll all go to check on the ponies and top up their hay and water. I know you love your ponies but they need to get their rest too. I expect everyone to be polite and helpful, to listen to what Saffy and I say, and to keep the barn and their stables tidy. The

schedule for each day's activities will be put
up on the board." She nodded towards a
pinboard. "When we've finished lunch, we'll
take the ponies out for a hack on the beach.

There'll be time this evening to explore the beach without your ponies as well. But for now, dig in!"

"Mum! The bedrooms!" Willow whispered.

"Oh yes," said Sue, picking up a clipboard. "We have some bedrooms for three and some for four. I'm afraid there's no swapping allowed. In Kingfisher – Natalie, Ruby, Priya and Daisy; in Blackbird: Owen, Tilly, Grace and Ryan; in Kittiwake: Alex, Imogen and Kalini; in Osprey: Zara, Daniela and Amara . . ."

Amara only just stopped herself from gasping out loud. *What?* she thought in dismay. *There must be some mistake. I can't share with Zara and Daniela. Summer camp is ruined!*

CHAPTER THREE

Kalini, Imogen and Alex were as shocked as
Amara. "Go and talk to Sue," urged Kalini.

Amara bit her lip. "She said there was
no swapping allowed." The bubbles of
excitement that had been fizzing inside her
at the thought of the week ahead felt like
they had suddenly popped. "There's nothing
I can do. I guess I'm with Zara and Daniela
whether I like it or not."

Imogen squeezed her arm. "Don't worry. If

it's anything like last year, we'll hardly be in the bedrooms."

"Yeah, and you can come into our room as soon as you wake up and stay in our room until it's lights-out each night," said Alex.

They're right, Amara told herself. *I only have to sleep in the same room as Zara and Daniela. It's not like I have to be with them the rest of the time.*

Kalini gave her a worried look. "Are you sure you don't want to talk to Sue about it?"

But Amara didn't want to make a fuss. "No, I'll be OK."

When they finished eating, they fetched their bags and Amara went to her room. Zara and Daniela had already bagged the two beds next to the window, leaving the bed that had no window for Amara.

"I can't believe we have to share with you," Zara said sourly.

"It wouldn't be my choice either," Amara retorted.

"I hope you don't snore," Daniela said.

"And you're not to touch any of our things!" said Zara.

Amara rolled her eyes. As if she'd want to touch any of Zara's and Daniela's things!

There was a knock on the door and Willow poked her head in. "Amara! Do you want company while you unpack?"

Amara smiled at her, relieved to see a friendly face. "Yes, please."

Willow bounced into the room. "Hi!" she said brightly to Zara and Daniela. They both gave her withering looks but Willow didn't seem bothered. "As soon as you've unpacked, let's go to the stables. I want you to meet Clown," she said to Amara. "He's been my pony since I was six."

"Cool!" said Amara. The less time she spent in the room with Zara and Daniela the better!

She threw her things into her chest of drawers. "OK, I'm done," she said to Willow a few minutes later.

As she walked past Zara, the blonde girl stuck her leg out, tripping her up. "Whoopsie!" she said as Amara fell over.

"Hey, that was mean!" said Willow angrily.

Daniela giggled. "Amara should get used to being on the floor. It's where she's going to end up when she has a jumping lesson!"

She and Zara sniggered.

Amara saw Willow start to frown and

grabbed her arm. "Let's go," she said. She didn't want to ruin her first day by getting into a row.

"They're horrible!" said Willow as she and Amara left the log cabin.

"I know," said Amara. "They live in Eastwall where I live."

"Are they always that mean?" asked Willow.

"Yep," sighed Amara.

Willow's green eyes sparkled mischievously. "Maybe I'll play some pranks on them."

"What kind of pranks?" asked Amara.

Willow grinned. "Oh, I know plenty. Just you wait and see!"

Clown was stabled in the separate old brick

stable block near the house along with a pretty grey horse and a large chestnut. "The grey is Tala; she belongs to Saffy," Willow explained. "The chestnut is Arty; he's Mum's." She passed an empty stable and then stopped at the end one which had a slightly lower door. "And this is Clown."

A little brown-and-white pony stuck his head over the door and Amara stroked him. He had large eyes and a heavy forelock. Willow opened the door – Amara noticed the bolts at the top of the stable doors were the same as the kick bolts at the bottom of the doors so they could be easily opened by pushing them up with one hand. Willow went into the stable and fussed over Clown, smoothing his mane and kissing his face. Amara could see she adored him.

"I need to give him a brush before we go out to the beach," said Willow. "I was too busy helping Mum get the barn ready this morning. Do you want to help me?"

"Sure," said Amara.

Willow fetched a headcollar and grooming kit. Amara watched as Clown lowered his head to make it easier for Willow to put the headcollar on him. She slipped it over his ears, did the buckle up and then tied him up to a metal ring in his stable wall. Then she grabbed a hoof pick. Amara wondered how she would pick out Clown's hooves. People usually used one hand to hold the pony's hoof up and the other hand to hold the hoof pick.

"Do you want some help with that?" she offered.

Willow flashed her a smile. "Thanks, but I can manage fine."

She tapped one of Clown's front legs. He lifted it obediently. Willow supported it between her left arm and her body as she used the hoof pick in her right hand to clean the dirt out of his hoof. Clown stood patiently. It was clear he had been very well trained.

When his hooves had been cleaned out, Amara and Willow set to work brushing him. As they worked, they chatted. Amara told Willow all about Moonlight Stables – missing out the fact that some of the horses there were magic, of course! Willow told her all about Seaview and what it was like living there.

Afterwards, they went to the main barn. Ember whinnied when he saw Amara and she felt her heart swell with love.

"He's gorgeous," said Willow, patting him.

Amara beamed. She loved it when people praised Ember.

They all got tacked up.

"Before we set off, there are a few things you need to know about riding on a beach," Sue explained. "It's important to always look at the tide times because when the tide starts to come in, it's very easy to get cut off from the routes back to the clifftop. You should also never just get on to the sand and gallop. Always walk and trot along it first and check the sand is safe before you gallop. Finally, you must look out for people walking or playing on the beach. Our beach is very quiet but if you do see anyone, give them plenty of room. Understand?"

They all nodded and then it was finally time to set off! Saffy led the ride on Tala and Sue brought up the rear on Arty. They rode down the long drive, before crossing the small road and heading on to a bridlepath that ran along the edge of some fields. As they got closer to the beach, seagulls circled overhead, calling out to each other, and

Amara could smell the salt even more clearly in the air. They crossed another small road and rode to the clifftop where a path led down to a wide sandy beach. The beach was split between the dry golden sand with its smattering of shells and shingle and the darker damp sand with pools of water.

"Later in the week we'll come back and you can take your horses for a swim," said Sue. "But today is just about riding on the sand."

"And galloping?" said Alex hopefully.

Sue smiled. "Yes, and galloping for those who want to. We'll ride along the sand together and then head back in two groups – those who want to stick to a trot and a slow canter can go first with Saffy and those who want to race can catch them up with me."

Amara didn't need magic to tell that

Ember was excited. His ears were pricked and he held his head high. He jogged and sidled sideways as his hooves met the sand. "Steady now," she soothed, patting him and remembering Sue's warnings. "We can't gallop yet."

I like it here, he told her.

Me too, she told him.

They reached the damp sand and trotted along it. On their right side was the sparkling sea and on their left side were high cliffs with caves and paths that led up to the clifftop.

Sue pointed out a patch of sinking sand they needed to avoid, marked by a red-and-white post – the sand looked just like normal sand but with a layer of water on the top. "Posts like that mark places where sinking sand often forms," said Sue. "Make sure you avoid going near them but also be aware that sinking sand can be anywhere, particularly after heavy rainfall or when the sand is waterlogged."

"What would happen if you went into it?" asked Kalini.

"The sand is very soft and it would close round the horse's legs," said Sue. "The more a horse struggles, the more the sand and water mix together and the quicker the horse sinks. They might not sink all the way in but they could get stuck and drown when the tide comes in."

Amara decided she was definitely going to avoid being anywhere near sinking sand!

Ember pulled at his bit, his neck starting to sweat with excitement. "Steady, boy," Amara soothed. Excitement swirled inside her at the thought of galloping but she knew they mustn't go until Sue said it was OK. She rode him towards the cliffs, trying to calm him down. As she did so, she heard a faint whinny from the caves at the bottom of the cliffs. Ember's ears pricked.

Did you hear that? he said.

Yes. Where did it come from? she said.

I don't know, Ember said. *But the horse sounds unhappy.*

Amara felt a prickle of concern. *Perhaps it's a pony in need of help.*

Hearing a shout, she looked around. Sue was beckoning to all the riders to join her.

"We're going to have to go," Amara said.

OK, Ember said reluctantly, but he looked round once more at the caves as they joined the others.

"Is everyone ready?" called Sue.

"Yes!" the riders cried.

"Then off you go!"

The ponies leapt forwards in a line. The six elemental horses – Ember, Tide, Rose and Thunder, along with the Storm Stables horses, Scorch and Quake – quickly shot into the lead. Even without being in their magical form they were still faster than normal ponies. The six of them raced across the sand, neck and neck. Crouched low over Ember's mane, Amara lost herself in the

exhilarating sensation of speed, the wind in her face dragging tears from her eyes as Ember's hooves drummed on the hard, damp sand.

She was on the outside of the group, nearest to the sea. On her left, Zara was urging Scorch on with her whip. From the determination on her face, it was clear she wanted to catch up with Saffy first. Scorch put her ears back and started to pull ahead.

But Ember was determined not to be beaten. His neck stretched out and he

matched Scorch stride for stride.

"Go, Ember!" Amara urged.

Zara shot a furious look at her and started to move Scorch towards Ember, pushing him in the direction of the sea and forcing him to slow down slightly. Zara's knees and stirrups knocked against Amara's.

"What are you doing?" Amara shouted.

"Amara!" Imogen yelled. "Look ahead of you!"

Amara saw to her horror that Zara had pushed her so far over to the right that she and Ember were now heading straight for the sinking sand that Sue had pointed out.

"Ember! Watch out!" she shrieked.

But Ember was galloping so fast he couldn't stop in time!

CHAPTER FOUR

Amara braced herself, expecting to hear the squishing sound of the soft waterlogged sand, but to her astonishment, the sand held firm. Ember slowed right down but then, realising he wasn't sinking, he picked up a canter again. Scorch and Quake had now surged on ahead of him so there was no chance of catching up.

What just happened? Amara's thoughts spun. Glancing to her left, she caught sight of Tide, who had slowed down to a trot while Imogen patted and praised her.

It was Tide, said Ember. *She used her magic to take the water out of the sand we galloped into.*

Kalini and Alex had slowed down too. "Are you OK?" Alex called.

"Yes," gasped Amara as her heart gradually stopped racing. In front of them, Zara and Daniela were high-fiving each other.

"We won!" crowed Zara.

"Pity your ponies are so slow," Daniela taunted the Moonlight Stables riders as they rode up to them.

"You almost pushed Amara into the sinking sand, Zara!" said Kalini. "It could have been really dangerous."

Zara shrugged. "She wasn't that near the

sinking sand. It was just race tactics."

"You're all just sore losers," said Daniela.

"They're losers full stop," sniggered Zara.

"Is everything OK here?" Saffy asked curiously, riding over to them.

"Yeah, fine," said Amara quickly as Sue and the rest of the riders reached them. She was cross with Zara but she knew there was no way to explain how the sinking sand Zara had forced them into had magically dried out.

Imogen rode up alongside her. Amara bent down. "Thanks, Tide," she whispered, stroking the pretty grey pony who was still puffing slightly.

Tide whickered softly.

"OK, everyone. Back to the yard!" called Sue.

She and Saffy led the ride up the cliff path. Ember paused at the bottom, looking back to the caves. Amara remembered the whinny they'd heard earlier. Where had it come from?

I'll tell the others about it when we get back, she decided.

Once the ponies were settled in their stables, Amara pulled Alex, Imogen and Kalini to one side and told them about the whinny she and Ember had heard. "It might be nothing but I think we should check it out when we go back to the beach without the ponies."

They nodded.

"If there's an unhappy horse, we need to help it," said Imogen.

"We'll explore the caves and see what we find," said Alex.

They all got changed and walked down to the beach. As Sue set up a beach volleyball game with Willow, Amara asked if it was OK if she and the others went and explored the caves.

"Sure, but we'll need to leave at about six before the tide comes in so keep an eye on the time," Sue said.

While the rest of the campers played volleyball or paddled in the sea, Amara and the others searched the caves. Near to where Ember had heard the whinny, they found a cave with some small hoofprints and a few long strands of white hair caught on a rock.

"It looks like a horse was definitely here," said Alex.

"I wonder what it was doing on its own," said Kalini.

"And where's it gone?" said Amara.

"Maybe it escaped from a field nearby and found its way home," suggested Imogen.

"Mmm," Amara said. She couldn't shake off the feeling that something was wrong. "Ember said it sounded frightened. What if it's still here somewhere? There are so many caves."

"We can't check them all," said Imogen.

"I know!" said Alex. "Let's bring Rose, Thunder, Ember and Tide here tomorrow morning before everyone else gets up and see if they can help us find it."

"That would mean breaking the rules," said Kalini slowly.

"We can make sure we're back by morning

feed time." Alex looked round at them.
"If there's a chance that there's a horse in trouble, we should try and find it. Who's going to come with me?"

Their eyes locked together. "Me!" they said.

That night, Amara reluctantly made her way to her bedroom. Daniela was in bed and Zara was putting strange fabric rollers in her hair.

"No snoring," Daniela said sourly to Amara.

Amara didn't bother to reply. She couldn't believe her luck that she had to share a room with the mean cousins. She wished she was with the others. She was sure they'd be whispering jokes and stories to each other . . .

HA-HA-HA!

She jumped as she heard a loud creepy laugh outside their window. She sat up and saw Zara and Daniela doing the same.

"What was that?" gasped Daniela, turning the torch on her phone on.

The noise came again, starting low and getting louder: *WHOOO-HA-HA-HA-HOOO.*

Amara's heart slowed down. She grinned, feeling she might just know what was going on. Getting out of bed, she padded to the window.

"What are you doing?" hissed Zara.

Amara pulled back the curtains.

A strange white face appeared on the other side of the glass. Zara and Daniela both screamed and hid under their duvets.

Amara opened the window. Willow was

crouching underneath it, holding up a cut-
out face on a stick while trying to smother
her giggles in her arm. On the grass next to
her, there was a plastic box with a button and
a picture of a laughing face on it. The strange
laughing sound was coming from it.

"Willow!" said Amara, laughing.

Behind her there were outraged squawks.

"It was a trick?"

"It was just Willow?"

Zara and Daniela jumped out of their beds and stormed over to the window.

"Hi!" said Willow, waving the face at them and grinning.

Zara folded her arms. "I'm going to tell."

"Me too!" said Daniela.

Just then there was a knock on their door and Saffy looked in. "What's going on in here?" She came to the window, saw Willow and rolled her eyes. "Oh, Willow, not the laughing ghost prank again," she sighed.

Willow chuckled. "Sorry, Saff. It has to be done. It's a first night ritual."

"Bed," said Saffy, pointing a finger at her. "Before I tell your mum."

"OK," said Willow, picking up the laughter box. "See you in the morning, Amara." She gave Zara a cheeky grin. "Cool curlers, Zara!"

Giggling, she ran off.

Zara scowled and swung round to Saffy. "Aren't you going to tell her off? She really scared us."

"We were terrified!" said Daniela.

"Of a strange laugh and a puppet on a stick?" said Saffy, her eyebrows rising. "Seriously, girls, I think you'll survive. Now, back to bed, all of you."

While Zara and Daniela whispered crossly to each other about how Willow should have been punished, Amara lay down and shut her eyes. She and the others had an early start in the morning.

I wonder if we'll find the horse, she thought as she drifted off to sleep.

CHAPTER FIVE

A faint pale grey light was peeping around the edges of the curtains when Amara woke up. She checked her phone. 5 a.m. exactly. She always woke up early when there was something important to do that day.

She pulled on her clothes and quietly let herself out of the bedroom, just as the others came out of their room too. They crept out of the cabin and ran to the barn. There was no need to tack up because they were going

to ride their horses in their elemental forms
to get to the beach more quickly. However,
Amara grabbed a headcollar and leadrope
just in case they did find a loose horse on the
beach.

As they rode away from the barn, Kalini
glanced round anxiously in the direction of
the log cabin and the farmhouse. "I hope no
one wakes up."

Amara was worried about that too. If they
were found getting the horses out at this time
of the morning, they'd be in serious trouble.
They couldn't exactly explain that it was OK
because the horses were magical.

Looking at Imogen biting her lip, she could
tell that she was concerned too.

Alex was the only one who didn't seem to
be worrying at all; his eyes were alight with

excitement. "Come on!" he said, pushing Rose into a canter. "Let's go!"

Once they were safely in the fields, all four horses transformed. Ember's mane and tail turned into flickering flames and his eyes glowed amber. Tide's coat turned a bluey-silver, her eyes becoming the turquoise of the sea on a summer's day and her mane and tail frothing like sea foam. Rose's mane and tail turned a mossy green, filling with wildflowers, and her chestnut coat gleamed with golden flecks. Thunder's mane and tail swirled around him like the wind, his dapple coat darkened and his eyes turned a deep coal black.

Whinnying in delight, the four horses set off across the fields towards the beach, their hooves moving so fast they hardly

touched the ground. Amara felt her worries fade away. It was impossible to think about anything apart from how amazing it was to be riding Ember in his elemental form.

It had taken ten minutes to ride to the beach that afternoon, but with magic it only took them two. They stopped at the top of the path. The tide was coming in, rolling closer to the rocks and caves. But on the broad strip of sand not yet covered by water, they saw a pale grey foal picking its way across the beach. It looked to be a year old. Its dark grey mane and tail were still quite short and bushy and its legs looked long compared to its slim body. Lifting its head, it whinnied, its call shrill and sad.

"There's the horse!" exclaimed Amara.

"Where has it come from?" said Kalini.

"And who does it belong to?"

"Maybe it's escaped from somewhere," said Alex.

"We can't just leave it here," said Imogen.

"Let's try and get the headcollar on it," said Amara. "Then we can take it back to the yard. We can tell Sue we found it on the drive."

They cantered down the cliff path and on to the sand but the foal plunged away. They followed it but that only made it go faster. Although they could have easily overtaken it as their horses were so much faster than the foal, they didn't want to scare it.

The foal stopped outside the caves, its eyes wary, its ears flickering as it looked at them.

"Let's gradually close in," said Alex.

"What about the tide?" said Amara, glancing back. The sea was coming in fast.

"We've got time," said Alex. "Spread out, everyone."

They did as he said. The foal whinnied anxiously and trotted into one of the caves.

"I'll try to get close with Tide," said Imogen, jumping off. "The rest of you stay here in case it bolts for freedom. Amara, can I have the headcollar and leadrope?"

"Sure." Amara handed it to her. Imogen pulled some horse treats from her pocket and headed into the cave with Tide. They stopped a little way in.

"It's OK, we're not going to hurt you," Imogen said soothingly. She held out the treats but the foal ignored them. Imogen glanced round at the others. "He seems really scared."

Tide whickered softly and stretched out

her nose. The foal hesitated and then gave a tentative whicker back.

Tide stepped forward. The two grey horses nuzzled noses and then Tide looked at Imogen and nodded.

Amara held her breath as Imogen approached slowly and stopped next to Tide. Tide whickered reassuringly to the foal as if to tell him that there was nothing to be scared of. This time when Imogen held out a treat, the foal took it and let her slip the

headcollar over its head.

Imogen gave the leadrope a gentle tug and the foal followed her and Tide out of the cave.

"Well done. Let's get him back to the stables," said Amara, but as she looked round, she caught her breath. Although the patch of beach they were standing on was still dry, the sea had come in on both sides and now instead of sand, there was just water stretching between them and the cliff path.

"How are we going to get back?" said Kalini, her eyes wide as she realised the same thing too.

Amara's heart sped up. The cliff face in front of them was much too steep to climb.

She could feel Ember trembling. Water was not his element and she could feel the fear running through him. She stroked him, trying to soothe him.

"Let's try and ride through it," said Alex, urging Rose towards the water. "It's not that deep yet and if it gets deep the horses can swim."

"Alex, no!" exclaimed Kalini. "If the ponies lose their footing, the waves will push us on to the rocks. It's too dangerous!"

"We can't just stay here and drown!" exclaimed Alex.

"Tide says she'll try and help," said Imogen. "Her powers work much better with fresh water but she's going to try and push the waves back for a short while so we can get to the path. Get ready to gallop!"

Tide stamped her front hooves on the sand and Amara felt the air crackle with magic. With a clatter of stones and shingle, the sea drew back, pulling away and leaving a small strip of damp sand from where they were standing to the bottom of the cliff path.

"You did it, Tide!" Alex whooped. "Come on, everyone!"

They set off at a gallop with the foal beside them but as they did so, Imogen gasped. "Tide's losing control of the magic!"

The water that had drawn back had curled into a massive wave. With a sudden roar, it came rushing towards them.

Amara felt fear surge through her as the wall of water bore down on them. There was no way of escaping. They were going to drown!

CHAPTER SIX

Amara braced herself for the cold water to hit them but suddenly the enormous wave exploded into millions of water droplets that shot up into the air and rained down on them.

Tide, thought Amara in relief, but the next second she realised Imogen and Tide were looking as shocked as everyone else. She turned to see the foal rearing up on his back legs. His coat was now gleaming pure silver and his eyes were glowing aquamarine. His once stubby mane and tail swirled around in long silver and white translucent strands. Tide hadn't stopped the wave – the foal had!

But there was no time to think about that now. "Come on!" Amara shrieked as the sea started to sweep in towards them again.

The others didn't need telling twice. Their horses leapt into a gallop, the foal keeping pace beside them as they raced over the damp sand and up the cliff path just as the sea came crashing back in against the rocks. The horses bolted up the stony track and only stopped when they reached the top.

Amara's heart was hammering in her chest, her breath coming in gasps and her wet hair was plastered against her face with sea water.

"That was close," said Alex. For once, even his voice sounded shaky.

The foal transformed back into his normal pony shape, his head hanging low as he gulped in air.

Imogen scrambled off Tide and stroked him. "It's OK," she soothed. "You're safe."

Despite her own tiredness, Tide stepped forward and nuzzled the foal, who looked at her gratefully.

"Tide says he's a Water Horse, just like her," explained Imogen. "But he's a Sea Horse so he's much better at doing magic with sea water. Tide can control all water but she finds it harder with sea water. She couldn't control the wave she made when she was trying to save us just now."

Kalini dismounted and went over to the foal too. "Thank you for helping us," she said softly.

The foal let them stroke his face and gently rub his ears.

"Do you have a home?" Imogen asked him.

The foal shook his head.

"We should tell Jill," said Kalini. "She'll know what to do."

"Let's stick with our plan of taking him to the stables," said Imogen. We can tell Sue we got up early to have a walk and saw him on the driveway, then we can phone Jill after breakfast."

They all nodded.

Tide gave the foal another nuzzle. His breathing had steadied now.

Aware that soon there might be early morning walkers around, the horses transformed into their pony shapes and they headed back across the fields, the foal beside them. As the minutes ticked past, Amara felt her stomach start to knot with tension. *Please let us get back before anyone realises we've been gone,* she thought. But as they turned into the yard, her heart sank. Sue was standing in front of the barn!

Amara exchanged dismayed looks with the others.

"Sue! We can explain!" Alex started to gabble. "I mean, actually we can't but . . . but . . ."

"In the barn, right now!" Sue said, striding towards them, her voice low and anxious. "And for goodness sake, don't let anyone see you!"

They swapped uncertain looks.

"Now!" she urged.

They jumped off and the ponies trotted beside them into the barn and into their stables. Amara's thoughts raced. *Why wasn't Sue more angry? Or more surprised?*

They bolted the ponies' doors and swung round to look at Sue. She had pulled the main barn door shut behind her and was holding the foal's leadrope.

"Can one of you please explain what's going on? And where this foal has come from?" She stroked him. "Another elemental horse if I'm not mistaken."

Their mouths dropped open. For a moment they were all so shocked, no one spoke.

"Um ..." Amara's mouth felt dry. She swallowed. "How do you know about ... about ..."

"About elemental horses?" Sue finished for her.

Amara nodded.

"I'm a True Rider," Sue said with a smile.

Amara felt the tension rush out of her.

"Jill and I were True Riders together when we were younger and she still had Shula, her elemental horse," Sue explained. "Ivy too until . . . well, until she became a Night Rider." She looked at the foal. "So, where has he come from?"

They quickly explained everything that had happened. "We were going to ring Jill and tell her about him," said Kalini.

"Good idea," said Sue. "I'll call her. I'm sure

she'll be happy to look after the foal until he's old enough to find his True Rider. But don't breathe a word to Zara and Daniela. Ivy will be bound to want him if she finds out he's an elemental."

"We'll keep his magic secret," promised Kalini.

Amara rubbed her head. It was brilliant that Sue was a True Rider and she wasn't going to send them home for breaking the rules, but she had so many questions. "If you're a True Rider, is Arty your elemental horse?" she asked, curiously.

"No," said Sue. "My elemental horse, Ocean, died peacefully of old age, six years ago. Elemental horses live longer than normal horses but sadly they don't live as long as humans."

Amara exchanged looks with the others. The thought of Ember dying was unbearable.

"How did you cope?" Kalini whispered, clearly thinking the same thing.

"I know you can't understand now but the time was right. Ocean and I had done so much, had so many adventures, but he was tired and I knew he was ready to pass on. I'm just grateful for the time we had together. You have to make the most of every moment you have with your elemental horses," she said softly. "And then, when the time comes, be brave and let them go."

They were all silent for a moment.

"Is . . . is Willow a True Rider?" asked Imogen.

"No," said Sue. "She doesn't know anything

about elemental horses. Please don't tell her."

"Why?" said Alex. "She's a Legacy Rider, she's allowed to know."

"Yes, but I don't want to tell her in case she's never chosen to be a True Rider. I had a friend like that," said Sue. "He knew about this amazing world of magic but he was never chosen and he became very bitter about it. Willow has enough challenges in her life. If an elemental horse finds her and chooses her then that will be the right time for her to know about all this."

Amara could just about understand. Since finding out about elemental horses, she'd sometimes wondered what it must be like to be a Legacy Rider who never became a True Rider. It would be awful to know about the magic and not be able to be part of it – far worse than never knowing.

Sue checked her watch. "We've got ten minutes until everyone else gets here for morning feed time. Why don't you go round the back of the barn and then join in with the others when they get here?"

They all nodded, and after giving their ponies one last pat, slipped out of the barn, leaving Sue with the foal.

"Wow!" Imogen breathed when they got outside.

"Sue's a True Rider," whispered Kalini.

"Luckily," said Alex. "I thought we were about to be sent home when we saw her standing there."

"Me too," said Amara. "I'm so glad she understands. We must keep the foal's secret."

"Yeah, Ivy mustn't find out!" declared Alex.

"Ivy mustn't find out what?" They all swung round. Zara and Daniela had rounded the corner of the barn without them noticing. "Well?" Zara said suspiciously. "What mustn't Ivy find out?"

Amara didn't know what to say.

"It's . . . um . . ." Imogen's eyes were wide behind her glasses. "Um . . ."

"It's nothing!" squeaked Kalini.

Zara and Daniela didn't look convinced.

"Oh, guuuuuys," said Alex with a dramatic groan. "We've been found out! I guess we might as well admit it now. We were planning to ask Jill to come down the night before the One Day Event and walk the cross-country course with us to give us some extra tips," he told Zara and Daniela. "We didn't want Ivy to find out in case she decided to do the same."

"Yeah, we really want to beat you," Amara jumped in, knowing that was guaranteed to get a reaction from the Storm Stables riders.

"Beat us? Dream on," retorted Daniela. "No advice Jill can give you will make that happen." She hooked her arm through Zara's. "Come on, let's go and see the ponies."

Zara nodded and walked off with her but as they went, she looked back, her eyes suspicious. Amara felt a shiver of foreboding run down her spine. She had a feeling that Zara hadn't bought Alex's story quite as completely as Daniela.

"Phew, that was close!" said Imogen. "We'd better be super careful from now on."

CHAPTER SEVEN

Amara and the others followed Zara and Daniela into the barn. A group of the other riders including Willow were fussing around the foal. His ears flickered nervously and his eyes darted from side to side.

"He's so cute."

"He's gorgeous."

"I can't believe you just found him wandering on the drive, Mum," Willow said.

"I'll have to try and find out where he's

come from," said Sue. "But for now, he can go in the stable block in the spare stable beside Clown."

"I'll take him," said Willow eagerly.

She reached for the leadrope and the foal started back. "It's OK, silly, I won't hurt you," Willow murmured to him. She waited patiently until he relaxed and then slowly stepped forward and rubbed his nose.

"Come with me," she told him, leading him out of the busy barn.

Amara and the others mucked out, filled their ponies' haynets, scrubbed and refilled their water buckets and then swept up all the loose straw. Then Amara helped some of the younger ones who were struggling. She was very used to helping out at Moonlight Stables and she was always happy to do pony chores. Daniela and Zara clearly felt differently.

"This wheelbarrow's too heavy," moaned Daniela. "And the straw smells."

"I don't want to sweep up. We usually have grooms to do things like that," Zara said crossly to Saffy.

"Well, we don't have any grooms here," said Saffy. "So, you'd better get sweeping."

The morning was a blur of activity. After breakfast, they had their first showjumping lesson. Saffy was a good teacher and explained things clearly, starting with the jumps very low and slowly building up the height.

Amara hadn't done much jumping. Most of the time at Moonlight Stables they practised mounted games and when she did jump, she usually just pointed Ember and hoped he would clear it. However, Saffy began to teach her how to control his speed and how to help him find the right stride into the fence so he could take off at the right place. By the end of the lesson she was jumping higher than she'd ever jumped before.

Willow and Kalini dropped out when
the fences were quite low but both of them
turned out to be really good when it came
to the dressage lesson later that morning.
Willow had done a lot of dressage before and
she and Clown clearly had an amazing bond.
She rode with both reins in her right hand
and directed Clown to change pace, turn,
stop or rein-back just by shifting her weight
slightly or pressing the reins against his
neck. Ember was too impatient to be good at
dressage – he kept wanting to canter when
he should be trotting and whenever he had
to stand still, he tossed his head and fidgeted.
By the end of the lesson, Amara had decided
she much preferred jumping!

Alex clearly felt the same. "Rose and I
really don't like dressage," he said when they

were untacking the ponies at the end of the morning.

"I guess that means you've given up on trying to beat us in the One Day Event," said Zara, walking past with her saddle.

"Yeah, because you have to do showjumping, cross country and dressage," said Daniela. "You can't just jump."

"I might not be able to beat you but I bet Immy will," Alex said. "Tide was brilliant at dressage. She and Immy looked as good as Malia and Goldie when they're doing dressage."

Imogen rolled her eyes. "Not quite," she said, but she looked pleased. "Tide does like it though. Me too."

"Your dumb pony is never going to beat Quake and Scorch!" said Daniela. "They're worth far more money than she is!"

She and Zara walked off.

"Oh, I really wish they weren't here!" Imogen exclaimed in annoyance.

Lunch was another big spread of sandwiches, crisps, salad and fruit. Before the chocolate brownies were served, Willow got up and left the table. She came back later just as they were clearing away.

"Where have you been?" Amara asked.

"I just remembered something I needed to do." Willow's eyes twinkled mischievously.

Amara studied her closely. She had the strong feeling that she was up to something.

"Do you want to come and help me with Wave once we've cleared away?" asked Willow. "I want to wash and groom him."

"Wave?" said Amara.

Willow nodded. "Mum said I could name the foal and the name Wave just popped into my head. What do you think?"

Amara smiled. "I think it's perfect!"

They went to Wave's stable. He was standing at the back and hearing them at the door, he jumped nervously.

"It's OK, boy," said Willow, unbolting the door. "It's just us."

She went in and the foal sniffed her outstretched hand. He stared at her with his coal-black eyes and then lifted his nose to her face and breathed out.

Willow gently blew back at him.

He nuzzled her hair.

"See, there's nothing to be scared of," she told him, fetching his headcollar.

They took him to the wash area outside

the barn and tied him up. After they had finished brushing him, they shampooed him.

They were just rinsing the shampoo out when Zara and Daniela came over.

"He's cute," said Daniela, almost smiling for once.

Amara felt a prickle of anxiety as she watched Zara give the foal a thoughtful look. All elemental horses were beautiful in their pony form. There was something about them that stood out – their eyes had a particularly intelligent expression, their coats shone and their manes and tails were soft and silky. Zara knew this just as well as Amara did and now the foal was clean and bathed, his beauty was even more obvious. "So, he just appeared on the driveway this morning?" Zara said to Willow.

"Yeah. Mum's rung round but she hasn't found anyone locally who's missing a foal. It's weird!"

"It is, isn't it," said Zara slowly.

Daniela stepped forward to stroke the foal but he shied back in alarm and to Amara's horror, the soapy water in the nearby bucket exploded upwards. She threw herself towards it, pretending to trip and knocking the bucket flying. The water splashed

towards Daniela and Zara.

"Amara!" Daniela exclaimed. "Seriously! Could you be any clumsier?"

"Sorry!" she said, picking herself up off the floor as Willow soothed the foal.

"My trainers are soaking now," Daniela moaned. "I'm going to have to change them."

"Mine too," said Zara crossly.

They stomped away. Amara drew in a breath. She'd stopped them from realising it had been the foal who had caused the water to go everywhere – but only just.

"Are you OK?" Willow asked her.

"Yeah, I'm fine," said Amara, stroking Wave, who nuzzled her. But anxiety stabbed through her. If Wave couldn't control his powers, she wasn't sure they'd be able to keep his magic secret for long!

CHAPTER EIGHT

After lunch, they all got ready to go on a woodland ride. But when they mounted their ponies, everyone started to shout and call out.

"My saddle feels wonky!"

"My stirrups are all wrong!"

"What's happened?"

Amara realised she had one stirrup that had been let really far down and one that was up so far, her leg was bent like a jockey's.

"Willow!" Sue said, fixing her with an exasperated look.

Willow's shoulders were shaking and she was covering her mouth with her little arm to smother her giggles.

"That's what you were doing at lunchtime!" Amara realised. "You were changing all our stirrups!"

"It feels really weird, doesn't it," said Willow through her giggles. "Try riding like that!"

They all had a go. Riders usually had their stirrups the same length so having one short and one long felt very strange. After a few minutes, they had all adjusted their stirrups, and they set off on the ride.

It was wonderful to canter along the leafy paths in the nearby woods. They saw squirrels and birds and even a couple of deer. They crossed a wide stream and stopped beside a beautiful waterfall. They finished by having a long gallop up a gently sloping track.

"I like galloping a lot more than dressage!" Alex said as he and Amara pulled Rose and Ember up at the end.

"Me too!" she agreed with a grin.

After the ride, they cleaned their tack – all apart from Zara and Daniela who bribed two of the younger girls with a big bar of chocolate to do theirs for them.

"If Saffy or Mum see, they'll get into trouble," said Willow as she watched them sunbathing together.

"I don't get it, it's fun doing things like cleaning tack," said Amara.

"Tell you what else is fun," said Alex, jumping to his feet with his clean bridle over his shoulder. "Jumping the cross-country course fences on foot. Shall we?"

"I'm too tired," said Kalini.

"And it's too warm," said Imogen.

"No, it's not. It'll be fun!" said Alex, who always seemed to have more energy than everyone else combined.

"Oh, all right then," Imogen agreed, and Kalini nodded. Amara jumped to her feet too.

When the other riders heard what they were doing, they all wanted to join in. All apart from Zara and Daniela.

"Why would you want to run round the cross-country course?" said Daniela, wriggling her toes in the sun.

"Running round jumps is so babyish," said Zara.

"Hey, Zara!" Alex exclaimed suddenly. "Watch out!" He pointed at her. "You've got a spider on you!"

"A spider! Where? Get it off! Get it off!" said Zara, jumping to her feet and leaping round, shaking herself.

Alex burst out laughing. "Just kidding!"
Willow high-fived him in delight.

Zara glared and flopped down on the grass.
"You're so dumb, Alex," she said crossly.

"Says the person who's scared of imaginary
spiders," he said. Everyone trooped off after
him, talking and laughing, leaving Daniela
and Zara behind.

Running round the cross-country course
gave them a chance to get a proper look at all
the jumps before their cross-country lesson
the next day. Each jump had three different
height options – very low, medium and high.
There were jumps made from telegraph
poles and hedges, jumps that looked like
tables and chairs, and a jump down a bank

into a pool of water. Amara couldn't wait to see what Ember thought of the jumps the next day!

As they walked round, Willow talked non-stop about Wave. Amara smiled at her. "You really like him, don't you?"

Willow nodded. "The vet came this afternoon and said he doesn't have a microchip. Mum says he may have just been dumped by someone who didn't want him." She gave Amara an excited look. "You know what I really, really want?"

"What?" said Amara.

"For Mum to say we can keep him. I mean, I know he'll be too young to be ridden until he's four years old but by then I'll have outgrown Clown and so maybe he could be my next horse. Wouldn't that be amazing?"

Amara swallowed. She didn't want to burst Willow's happy bubble but they'd had a text from Jill earlier, telling them she'd spoken to Sue and she was going to collect Wave at the end of the week when she picked them up.

"Yeah, I guess it would be," she said awkwardly. "Um . . . maybe you should talk to your mum."

Willow nodded. "I will. I'll talk to her tonight."

They got back to the yard just before the evening stable inspection.

"Let's do one last check of the ponies," said Imogen.

Going into the barn, they stopped dead. On the Blue Troop's side, the aisle was covered with bits of hay and straw. Grooming kits and mucking out tools had been knocked over and were scattered around. The other side of the aisle – the side that belonged to the Red Troop – was still perfectly clean and tidy.

"What's happened?" said Amara in dismay.

"Pranked you!" said Zara, jumping out of the tack room with Daniela.

"This isn't a funny prank!" exclaimed Willow. "Now the Blue Troop will lose loads of marks!"

"Oh dear, what a shame," said Daniela, not sounding like she cared at all.

"That was a really horrible thing to do," said Imogen.

"Chill, you're in our troop," said Zara. "We want to beat them, remember?"

"Not by doing this," said Alex.

"Wow, some people really can't take a joke," said Zara, snarkily.

Willow rounded on her. "There are funny jokes and there are mean jokes. This was mean!"

Everyone else muttered in agreement.

Rolling their eyes, Zara and Daniela

flounced out of the barn.

Luckily, with everyone helping, the Blue Troop's side of the barn was tidy and clean again by the time Sue and Saffy came out with their clipboards to check the stables and the barn.

Amara, I need to talk to you. Amara glanced round at Ember as she went to stand by his stable. His eyes were worried. *It's about Zara and Daniela.*

I know. What they did was really horrible, Amara thought back.

It's not about that. It's about the foal.

Amara felt a jolt of alarm. *What about him?*

When they came in here to mess things up, they were talking about him. They were wondering if he was an elemental horse.

No! Amara thought in dismay.

I heard them say they were going to spy on him and see if he does any magic.

Amara caught her breath. But just then Sue and Saffy arrived to inspect her stable so she smiled and pretended everything was OK.

"Full marks," said Sue after she had finished looking at Ember's clean stable.

"Thanks," Amara smiled. But inside her head, her thoughts were racing.

As Sue and Saffy continued to the next stable, she turned to Ember.

I'll tell the others. We'll come up with a plan.

Ember's eyes met hers. *We'll keep the foal safe, won't we?*

We'll try our best, Amara said.

After the inspection had finished, Amara got the others to go into the orchard with her and when she was sure there was no one anywhere near, she told them what Ember had told her.

They all looked worried. "We'll have to make sure Wave doesn't do any magic in front of them," said Imogen.

Amara remembered how the water had leapt out of the bucket at lunchtime. "He might be able to control the ocean but he doesn't have much control over fresh water," she said.

"It's only until the end of the week," Kalini said. "Then he can come home with us."

"That's another thing." Amara told them

what Willow had said to her on the cross-country course. "She really wants to keep him."

Imogen sighed. "I wish she could but I can't see Sue letting her."

"I know, and she's going to be so upset when he goes," said Amara, really wishing there was something they could do.

They all headed back to the main barn for supper. Just as they arrived, Amara noticed Willow running from the house towards the stable block where Wave was. Even from a distance, Amara could tell she was upset.

"I'll be back in a couple of minutes," she said to the others.

She slipped out of the room and hurried to the stables. The sound of crying was coming from Wave's stable.

"Willow?" she said, going to the door. Willow was standing in the semi-darkness, hugging Wave.

Seeing Amara, she hastily rubbed at her eyes with her arm.

Amara's heart went out to her. "So, your mum didn't say you could keep him?"

"No." Willow sniffed. "She said he's going to go to your stables."

Amara sighed. "I'm sorry. You can always come and visit though."

Willow swallowed a sob. "It won't be the same." She turned back to Wave and stroked his forehead. "I know he's only been here since this morning but I just feel like he belongs here with me. I . . ." she broke off and buried her face against his neck. "I can't explain it."

She didn't need to. It was exactly how Amara had felt when she'd first met Ember. She desperately wanted to help Willow keep Wave. "Wait here," she said.

She hurried to the farmhouse and knocked on the door. Sue opened it. "Amara? Is everything OK?"

"It's Willow," said Amara.

Sue sighed. "Is this about keeping Wave?"

Amara nodded. "Can't you keep him here? Tell Willow about elemental horses and see if he chooses her when he's older?"

"But what if he doesn't?" Sue shook her head. "She'll be devastated."

"Well, can't you just keep him here and not tell her about elemental horses?" said Amara.

Sue sighed. "Amara, can you honestly

imagine Wave being able to keep his magic secret from her for three more years?"

Amara wanted to say yes, but she knew Sue was right. Wave had lost control of his magic once already that day. If Willow was looking after him, she'd be bound to find out about him and if she did, it would be awful if he didn't choose her.

"I can't risk it," Sue said softly.

Amara nodded. She did understand. But it was just so hard on Willow.

"I'll bring her to visit," Sue said. "She can see him every few months and then if he chooses her when he's old enough, he can come back here." She gave Amara a sad smile. "I'm sorry, Amara. That's all I can do."

CHAPTER NINE

Over the next few days, as well as lessons and rides on the beach, they went swimming in the sea, toasted giant marshmallows over a campfire, played rounders and did a showjumping competition on foot. Imogen discovered Tide had a real talent for dressage and spent a lot of time practising the dressage test on foot and phoning Malia for tips. Kalini spent much of her spare time with her nose in horse books preparing for the daily dinnertime equestrian quizzes, whilst Alex thought up fun non-riding competitions for everyone to do – water fights, obstacle races and beach volleyball.

Amara spent a lot of her spare time with Willow and Wave, trying to hide the moments he lost control of his magic and made any water near him leap into the air. She ended up pretending to kick over a lot of buckets!

Willow started teaching Wave voice commands and led him round to let him investigate things he found scary. She was brilliant with him, staying very calm and never getting frustrated when he didn't understand. Sometimes, it was hard to believe she was only ten. She was very persistent and patient, and Amara noticed how Wave's eyes lit up whenever he saw her.

On Friday – the day before the Summer Camp One Day Event Showdown – the riders were given the afternoon to get their ponies ready for the competition. The barn and the washing area were hives of activity.

Willow brought Wave out from his stable and led him towards the other horses. "What are you doing?" Amara called.

"I thought he could come and watch what's going on," said Willow. "It'll be good for him."

Amara felt a stab of anxiety. There was a lot of water around – people were carrying buckets and using hosepipes. "Are you sure it's not too busy?"

"He needs to get used to things," said Willow, tying him up.

Wave watched everything warily, tensing whenever there was an unexpected noise like someone dropping a bucket. Amara tensed whenever he did, her eyes darting round in case magic happened. She was just starting to hope it might be OK when a group of younger girls started a water fight. Everyone joined in and soon there were sponges flying everywhere and people laughing and shrieking. Wave started to pace around anxiously at the end of his leadrope.

"Willow, I think he's getting upset!" Amara called. Willow turned to look and at that moment, Zara turned the hose she was holding on full, aiming the jet straight at Willow. It hit the back of her legs, making her cry out and stumble forward.

Wave whinnied shrilly. The jet of water

from the hosepipe arched backward and hit
Zara straight in the face.

"No!" gasped Amara as Zara spluttered and shrieked. She dropped the end of the hosepipe in shock. It writhed on the ground like a snake, spraying water over everyone.

Amara's heart sank as she saw Zara stare at Wave, realisation dawning in her eyes.

Not even bothering to turn the hosepipe off, she hurried away, pulling her phone from her pocket.

No, no, no, no, no, thought Amara. She had a feeling she knew exactly who Zara was about to phone!

As soon as Amara could, she got the others on their own and told them what had happened.

"This isn't good," said Alex.

"Let's not panic," said Imogen, adjusting her glasses. "Even if she's told Ivy, it's the competition tomorrow. Lots of people will be here. Ivy can hardly steal the foal in front of everyone."

"That's true," said Kalini. "If we see anything suspicious, we can tell Jill and Sue. They won't let Ivy take him."

Amara knew what they said made sense but her stomach wouldn't stop twisting itself into anxious knots. Once Ivy knew about Wave, Amara had a feeling she'd stop at nothing to steal him.

Kalini squeezed her hand. "It'll be OK."

Amara really hoped she was right!

When the ponies were bathed and plaited, everyone cleaned their tack. Everyone apart from Zara and Daniela of course, who once again bribed some of the younger girls to do the job for them. They sat in the sun, whispering to each other and reading messages on their phones. Amara really didn't like the air of bubbling excitement that surrounded them. They were planning something, she was sure.

When their tack was spotless, they walked the showjumping and cross-country courses one final time, trying to work out where they would jump each fence, and then Imogen insisted on running through the dressage test on foot.

"I don't know why you're bothering," Zara called to her. "Tide knocked three jumps down in our last practice. She's rubbish compared to Scorch and Quake. The first and second place rosettes are ours!"

"Ignore her," Amara said to Imogen as Zara walked off.

Imogen sighed. "Scorch and Quake really are brilliant at dressage, showjumping and cross country. They probably will win."

"So what?" Kalini said, slipping her arm through hers. "We'll enjoy the day far more than they will and at the end of it, even if we knock every fence down and forget our dressage tests, we're taking the best ponies home. I definitely wouldn't swap Thunder for either Scorch or Quake, all they ever do is bite and kick."

Imogen swapped smiles with her. "You're right," she said. "We do have the best ponies, no matter what. Tomorrow, I'm just going to go out and have fun!"

Amara stayed in the others' bedroom until lights-out as usual. When she went to her own room, she braced herself expecting a load of annoying comments from Zara and Daniela but to her surprise, they were already asleep.

Weird. They normally stayed up whispering and going on their phones. Maybe they just wanted to get a good night's sleep before the competition? Suspicion crept through her. Or maybe they were planning something . . .

Amara slept fitfully. She was in the middle of dreaming about riding on the beach with Ember when he suddenly stopped running and started whinnying. She woke up, and laying there, realised the whinnying wasn't just in her dream! She could only hear it faintly but she knew, beyond doubt, that it was Ember. She sat up. Glancing across at Zara's and Daniela's beds, her stomach felt as if it had been filled with ice cubes. They were empty. Zara and Daniela had gone!

Amara grabbed her phone and checked the time. 4.45 a.m. She leapt out of bed and threw on some clothes then she ran silently along the corridor to the others' room. The dark of night was only just starting to fade to the grey of dawn.

"Wake up!" she hissed, shaking them all. "Zara and Daniela have disappeared. I bet they're trying to take Wave!"

Five minutes later, the four of them were running to the stable block. Amara caught her breath. Wave's door was wide open and he was no longer inside.

"Quick! Let's get the horses!" said Imogen.

They sprinted to the barn. Ember, Tide, Thunder and Rose were whinnying and stamping their hooves.

Amara! Daniela and Zara took Quake and Scorch out about fifteen minutes ago, Ember said.

Amara opened his door and vaulted on to his back. The others did the same. As they emerged on to the yard, they saw a figure in pyjamas and trainers running towards them. It was Willow!

"Wave's gone!" She skidded to a halt as she noticed they were all sitting on their ponies bareback and bridleless. "What . . . what are you doing?"

"There isn't time to explain," said Amara.

"Stay here. We're going to find out what's

happened to Wave," said Imogen.

"I'm not staying here!" Willow exclaimed hotly.

"Please, Willow . . ." Kalini began but Willow was already running back up the yard.

"Come on, let's go!" Alex urged.

With Willow nearby they didn't dare let their horses change into their magical form. They cantered out of the yard and down the lane.

"Wait!" Hearing a shout, they looked round and saw Willow coming after them on Clown. She had put his headcollar on and was using his leadrope as a single rein. "I'm coming with you!"

There wasn't time to argue.

They all raced down the drive together. As

they reached the road, Amara saw something that sent a jolt of fear through her. Parked in a nearby layby was a gleaming black horsebox with a lightning flash on its side. The ramp was down and Zara and Daniela were trying to tug Wave inside whilst Ivy swished a whip behind him. He was leaning back on his haunches, his front legs planted

firmly on the ground.

"Get on there, you stubborn mule!" Ivy hissed, swiping at him with her whip.

"Don't you dare hit him!" shrieked Willow. She threw herself off Clown and charged at Ivy. She jumped up and grabbed the whip, trying to yank it out of Ivy's hand.

In their shock, Zara and Daniela loosened their hold on Wave's leadrope. He shook his head and the rope flew out of their hands. With a shrill whinny, Wave wheeled round and galloped across the road, and away down the side of the field, heading towards the beach.

"Get that foal!" Ivy screamed furiously at Zara and Daniela. "Don't let him escape!"

CHAPTER TEN

Zara and Daniela ran to Scorch and Quake.

"Change, Ember!" cried Amara. She'd have to deal with Willow seeing him later.

With a whinny, Ember transformed, his mane and tail turning to red and gold flames and his body becoming more muscular.

His hooves flew over the ground. Amara thought they'd catch up with the foal in seconds but then she saw him ahead of them, his mane and tail streaming out behind him like sea foam, his coat a glittering silver. He'd changed into his magical form too and though he wasn't as strong and powerful as Ember he was incredibly fast.

Hearing a thunder of hooves behind her, she glanced round and saw that she was being chased by Zara and Daniela on Scorch and Quake. Tide, Thunder and Rose were close on their heels with Clown a little further behind.

Amara and Ember reached the top of the cliff just in time to see Wave racing on to the sand. The tide was coming in and the sand was covered with pools of water.

Quake and Scorch shot past Ember and reached the beach first. The foal had the sea behind him. He reared up, striking out defiantly with his hooves as if daring them to come closer.

Quake stamped his hooves on the sand.

What's he doing? Amara asked Ember as Thunder, Tide and Rose pulled up beside them at the top of the path.

He's using his power to cause earthquakes to try and scare the foal, said Ember as the sand on the beach between Quake and Wave began to tremble and shake, the tremors running from Quake's hooves towards Wave like snakes slithering over the sand. The foal whinnied in alarm.

But Quake hadn't realised that making the sand shake would mix it with all the water on top and turn it into sinking sand. Wave saw what was happening and raced into the sea. Quake and Scorch tried to charge after him but their hooves plunged into the sinking sand. They bucked and kicked but they sank down – fetlock then knee then hock deep . . .

Zara and Daniela screamed and shouted as their horses panicked. The foal galloped through the waves and emerged on to firm sand a little way off, but Quake and Scorch were trapped in the deadly sinking sand and the harder they tried to get out, the faster they sank.

"We need to help them!" cried Kalini as Wave trotted back to the safe the cliff path.

Amara's heart raced. "Imogen, can Tide do something?"

"There's a lot of water in that sand; she's not sure she can control it all!" said Imogen.

Just then, Willow came galloping up on Clown. She saw what was happening. "I'll call Mum! She'll ring the coastguard."

"There isn't time!" said Imogen as the waves swept closer to Scorch and Quake and their riders. "Tide, please try and do something!" she begged.

Rearing up, Tide slammed her hooves down into the sand. There was a moment's pause and then suddenly it was as if a hoover was vacuuming up the water in the sinking sand. The magic sucked the water out of the sand, shooting it out into the sea. The horses stopped floundering as the sand suddenly

became firm under their feet.

"You did it, Tide!" cried Imogen.

"That was brilliant!" exclaimed Alex.

"Well done, Tide!" said Kalini.

"But how ... what ..." Willow stammered in astonishment.

Amara grinned at her. There was no point trying to keep the horses' secret now. "Magic," she said.

Willow's eyes widened to the size of dinner plates. "Oh!"

Quake and Scorch stood panting on the sand. They were coated from ears to tail with gloopy sand but at least they – and their riders – were safe. But then Amara noticed something.

"The sea!" she gasped, pointing.

The water that had been sucked from the

sand was gathering into an enormous wave. As they watched, it grew bigger and bigger.

"Get off the beach!" Alex yelled to Daniela and Zara.

Quake and Scorch turned to flee but they were both tired from struggling with the sinking sand and they didn't move fast enough. The wave started to rush towards them, a towering wall of water.

Tide stamped her hooves desperately but nothing happened. She couldn't control the ocean and the waves. Zara and Daniela cried out in fear.

On the path up to the clifftop, the foal stamped his hooves too but the wave didn't explode this time. It was too large. It started to break, its foaming top curving over above Quake and Scorch . . .

CHAPTER ELEVEN

A loud whinny rang through the air. The foal reared up, balancing on his back legs. He was stunningly beautiful in his magical form. His eyes glowed aquamarine and his pure white mane and tail swirled around him. He struck out with his front legs and whinnied again, the sound commanding and insistent. The enormous wave seemed to freeze in place. The water foamed and rippled but didn't fall.

Zara and Daniela clapped their heels to

their horses' sides, and Quake and Scorch found the energy to gallop out from under the deadly canopy of water. They charged up the path, sending stones scattering. When they were safely at the top, the foal landed on all four feet again. As his hooves touched the ground, the wave crashed down with a thundering roar, dumping tonnes of water on the sand where Scorch and Quake had been standing just a few seconds before.

Amara's breath left her in a rush.

"Wave's a magic horse too?" Willow gasped

as the foal gave a proud whinny and turned back into his pony form. He trotted the rest of the way towards them, his eyes sparkling.

"He is," said Amara as the other horses whickered and touched noses with him.

Willow dismounted and went over to Wave. He lifted his muzzle to her face. "I knew there was something special about you," she whispered.

Amara, Ember said suddenly. *Zara and Daniela are escaping!*

Looking round, Amara saw Quake and Scorch cantering away across the clifftop. "Let them go," she said. "The important thing is they didn't steal Wave."

"We need to get him home," said Imogen. "When horses like ours use their magic, they get tired," she explained to Willow.

"Particularly when they're young. He's still excited at the moment from using so much power but he'll soon feel tired and very weak."

Willow used a boulder to get back on Clown. "I want to know everything. I can't believe magic is real. That your horses and Wave are magic!"

"We'll tell you about it on the way back," said Alex.

They set off back to the stables together, telling Willow about elemental horses and True Riders.

"I can't believe Mum didn't tell me," Willow said slowly.

"I think she thought it would be really hard for you to know about if you never became a True Rider," Amara said, wondering if

Willow would be cross with her mum, but Willow seemed to understand.

"I get it." Willow looked at Wave walking beside Tide. "But now I know I want him to stay more than ever. Even if he doesn't choose me to be his True Rider, I want to be able to look after him and help him for as long as I can." The foal stumbled. When they'd set off from the beach, he'd been lively and excited but now his head was starting to droop and his hooves were starting to drag.

"Is he going to be OK?" Willow said anxiously.

"We're almost back," said Kalini. "Then he can rest."

Ivy's horsebox had gone from the layby. They crossed the road and headed up the drive. As they did so, Sue came driving down

it in her car. Seeing them, she slammed on the brakes and jumped out.

"What's going on?" she demanded, her face pale with worry. "When I woke up, I looked out of my window and saw Wave's door open. Then I found that you were missing from your room," she said to Willow. "Where have you all been?"

"At the beach," Willow burst out. "Zara and Daniela tried to steal Wave. That instructor of theirs – Ivy – was here with her horsebox. Wave escaped but then there was sinking

sand and a massive wave and magic and I
know all about elemental horses now . . ."

She broke off as Wave suddenly collapsed,
his slender legs buckling underneath him.

"Mum!" Willow gasped. "Help him!"

Sue didn't ask any more questions about
what they'd been doing. All her attention
was focused on the weak foal. Telling them
to stay with him, she turned the car round
and drove quickly back to the yard, then
returned a few minutes later with a blue
bottle and a syringe. She filled the syringe
and put it in the foal's mouth. "It's a tonic
made from coastal herbs," she said as she
squirted the contents into his mouth. "It
revives horses who have sea magic. I had it

for Ocean, my old horse."

They waited anxiously. They had all dismounted, the horses turning back to their pony form. Amara and the others crouched around Wave while their horses nuzzled him and Willow stroked his ears. After a few minutes, he lifted his head.

"He's starting to get some strength back," said Sue. "Let's get him back to his stable."

They helped support him as he stood up and then with Tide pressed close on one side and Rose on the other, they encouraged him step by slow step back to his stable. Once inside, he collapsed on the straw. Willow cupped her hands and offered him water from his water bucket. He drank gratefully.

"I'm going to make him a special mash – a warm feed with treacle and some more tonic that will help him get his energy back," Sue said.

"I'll stay with him," said Willow.

The others led their ponies back to the barn, brushed the sand off them, picked out the stones and dirt from their hooves, checked them over for scratches and injuries and refilled their haynets.

That was a very exciting adventure, Ember said, nuzzling Amara.

I'm really glad we had Tide and Wave's magic, Amara said, hugging him. In the stable across the aisle she could hear Imogen praising Tide and telling her how amazing she was.

What do you think will happen to Wave now? Ember asked. *Will Sue still send him home with us?*

I don't know. After everything that had just happened, Amara wanted Wave to stay at Seaview more than ever.

The friends finished tending to their horses and then made their way to Wave's stable. Wave was lying down and Willow was sitting with him. There was an empty feed bucket next to them and Wave's head was resting on her lap. Willow was singing softly to him and his eyes were closed.

Sue put a finger to her lips and quietly came out of the stable. She beckoned to them to follow her into the farmhouse. They walked into the cosy kitchen with its flagstone floor and scrubbed pine table. "OK," she said, fixing them with a look. "Now I want to know exactly what's going on!"

CHAPTER TWELVE

Amara and the others told Sue everything.
As Sue listened, her eyes darkened. "I'll
go and check Quake and Scorch and then
phone Ivy. She can collect Zara and Daniela
before breakfast. I don't want them here for
a second longer." She looked at the clock on
the wall. "It's still an hour till morning feed
time. Why don't you go and get some rest?
Amara, if one of the others doesn't mind
sharing their bed with you, you can move in

with them for now."

"You can top and tail with me," said Kalini quickly.

Amara heaved a sigh. "Thanks."

"What's going to happen to Wave?" asked Imogen.

"I don't know," said Sue, glancing out of the window towards the stable block. "It's going to be even harder for Willow to say goodbye now she knows Wave's an elemental horse but if he stays, there's no guarantee he'll choose her to be his True Rider and how will she cope with that?"

"She told me she'll accept it if Wave doesn't choose her," said Amara. "She just wants to have any time with him that she can."

Sue looked torn. "I don't know. It might be best for Wave to be with your horses – other elementals – learning from them."

"No," Imogen said. Sue looked at her in surprise. "When we got back, I was talking to Tide about him and she told me she thinks he should stay here by the sea," Imogen went on. "Tide's own magic works best with fresh water but Wave's power is over the ocean. Tide says the right place for him is here with Willow, not with us – not miles away from the sea."

"Tide really thinks that?" Sue said slowly.

Imogen nodded.

Sue paused and then smiled. "Well, who am I to argue with a Water Horse? If that's what Tide thinks, and Willow understands that there's no guarantee she'll be his True Rider, then Wave can stay." She saw them exchange delighted looks. "Go and tell

Willow and I'll check on Quake and Scorch?'

Amara and the others sprinted to the stable block. Wave lifted his head as they appeared in the doorway. "What is it?" Willow said, seeing their excited faces.

"Wave can stay!" Imogen burst out.

"You're going to be able to look after him just like you wanted," said Amara.

Willow stared. "Mum actually said that?"

"Yes!" said Alex.

Happy tears filled Willow's eyes and she threw her arms round Wave's neck. "Wave, did you hear? You don't have to leave! I know you might not choose me to be your True Rider but that's OK. At least I get to look after you for now."

Watching Wave gently nuzzle away the tears on Willow's face, his dark eyes shining,

Amara thought that Willow needn't worry, she was pretty sure Wave had already made up his mind about who his True Rider was going to be.

"Go on, Tide!"

"You can do it, Immy!"

Amara, Alex and Kalini sat with Jill, cheering on Imogen as she rode into the showjumping ring on Tide. They'd got the top mark in the dressage test and done a clear round on the cross-country course. If they could just go clear in the showjumping, they'd win the Summer Camp One Day Event Showdown.

Amara had been so tired from the morning that she'd jumped the wrong course in the cross country, and Alex had gone so fast in the showjumping he had knocked four fences down. Kalini had jumped far more carefully and had done well in the dressage but Thunder had got time faults on both jumping courses. None of them minded not being in the running for a rosette though – even Alex, who was usually super competitive. After the excitement of the morning, they were all so glad that Wave was safe and staying here with Willow that nothing else mattered.

Willow had decided not to compete Clown after his early morning gallop and she now stood with one arm over Clown's neck and one arm over Wave's, a picture of perfect happiness as she watched Imogen cantering Tide towards the first fence.

Tide jumped a beautiful clear round and as she galloped through the finish, all the other riders and their parents erupted into cheers.

"She won!" whooped Alex, high-fiving Amara.

"Way to go, Imogen!" shouted Amara.

"Well done, Tide!" cried Kalini as Imogen cantered round, beaming and patting Tide over and over again.

"Isn't it brilliant not to have Zara and Daniela here?" said Amara with a happy sigh as Imogen rode out of the ring. "I bet Tide would still have beaten them but this way we don't have to listen to their mean comments."

Sue had kept to her word and once she had checked that Quake's and Scorch's injuries were only minor, she called Ivy and told her to come and collect them.

Zara and Daniela had skulked off the yard, throwing their things into the horsebox as Ivy yelled at them. All the other riders had whispered and gossiped about why they'd been sent home, wondering whether it was because they'd been bribing other people to do their chores or because they'd been rude or unkind.

Amara and the others kept the truth firmly to themselves but it had been a massive relief to see the Storm Stables horsebox pull away and to enjoy the last day of their holiday without Zara's and Daniela's snide remarks.

Imogen came back into the ring and was presented with the trophy for winning the competition and then, along with the other rosette winners, she and Tide did a lap of

honour as everyone
cheered.

Afterwards, they
took the ponies into
the orchard to graze.
The parents organised
a barbecue while Sue
awarded the Blue
Troop the trophy for
getting the most points in the week and then
gave out mini trophies to everyone.

Alex's was for being the most energetic
person at camp, Kalini's was for being best at
quizzes, Imogen's was for being the person
who practised hardest and Amara's was for
being the most improved at showjumping.
Willow was given a trophy for being the
person who played the best pranks.

"Yet again," her mum said with a sigh.

Willow grinned. "I've got a whole shelf of these!" she said to Amara.

It didn't surprise Amara at all!

"I'm so proud of you all," said Jill, hugging them as Amara returned to the group. "Both as True Riders and as normal riders." They'd told her everything that had happened. "Sue says you've been amazing and she'll happily have you to stay any time."

"That's good," said Amara grinning. "Because we definitely want to come and visit Wave and Willow."

"Every summer," said Imogen.

"That suits me!" said Willow, overhearing.

After the presentation, they put the ponies in the barn and ate hot dogs and burgers along with coleslaw and corn on the cob.

Then Saffy put some music on and they all danced and sang together as the sun set. It was the perfect end to the perfect holiday. When the grey of twilight started to turn to the dark of night and the stars began to glitter in the sky, Amara and the others walked arm in arm down to the barn to say a last goodnight to the ponies.

Ember's eyes lit up as Amara ran over to him. She let herself into his warm stable and hugged him. "This has been the best holiday ever," she whispered. "Have you enjoyed it, Ember?"

He nuzzled her. *I enjoy everything when I'm with you.*

Amara kissed his forehead. Tomorrow they'd be heading home. But the holidays weren't over; the rest of the summer stretched out before them – helping Jill at the stables, practising for mounted games competitions, hanging out with her friends, stopping Ivy if she decided to cause any more trouble and doing lots of magic with Ember. She was so lucky to be a True Rider!

We're going to have so many more adventures together, aren't we? said Ember, reading her thoughts.

Definitely, she replied with a smile.

The End

True Rider: Amara Thompson

Age:
10

Appearance:
Brown hair and blue eyes

Lives with:
Parents

Best friend:
Kalini

Favourite things to do:
Anything with horses, drawing and reading pony stories

Favourite mounted game:
Bending race

I most want to improve:
Vaulting on and off at speed and getting my handovers right

Elemental Horse: Ember

Colour:
Black

Height:
14.1hh

Personality:
Loving, lively, hot-tempered

Pony breed:
Welsh section B x Thoroughbred

Elemental appearance:
Golden eyes, swirling mane and a magical, fiery tail

Elemental abilities:
Fire Horse - Ember can create fires, make things burst into flame and cast fire balls from his hooves

True Rider: Imogen Fairfax

Age:
10

Appearance:
Light brown hair and hazel eyes

Lives with:
Mum, Dad, two brothers Will (17)
and Tim (15), Minnie our cockapoo

Best friend:
Alex

Favourite things to do:
Anything with horses, walking
Minnie, helping at my gran's
teashop

Favourite mounted game:
Mug shuffle

I most want to improve:
My accuracy in races

Elemental Horse: Tide

Colour:
White-grey

Height:
14.1hh

Personality:
Thoughtful, sensitive and kind

Pony breed:
Arab x Welsh

Elemental appearance:
Blue eyes, silver-blue coat and a
flowing sea foam mane and tail

Elemental abilities:
Water Horse - Tide can make
it rain and manipulate bodies
of water to create waves,
whirlpools and waterspouts

True Rider: Alex Brahler

Age:
11

Appearance:
Black hair and dark brown eyes

Lives with:
Mum, Dad, sister Frankie
(15) and our chocolate Labradors,
Scooby and Murphy

Best friend:
Imogen

Favourite things to do:
Anything with horses, playing
football, cross-country running,
climbing and swimming

Favourite mounted game:
Five-flag race

I most want to improve:
Being more patient in
competitions so I'm not
eliminated by starting races
before the flag falls!

Elemental Horse: Rose

Colour:
Bright chestnut with flaxen
mane and tail, a white blaze
and four white socks

Height:
14.2 hh

Personality:
Patient, calm, confident

Pony Breed:
Welsh section C

Elemental appearance:
Bright green eyes, a mossy green
mane and tail covered in flowers

Elemental abilities:
Earth Horse - Rose can make plants
and flowers grow

Night Rider: Zara Watson

Age:
11

Appearance:
Blonde hair and green eyes

Lives with:
Mum most of the time
and Dad some of the time

Best friend:
Daniela (my cousin)

Favourite things to do:
Riding, playing tennis, shopping,
pamper sessions

Favourite mounted game:
Bottle race

I most want to improve:
Nothing, I'm good at everything

Elemental Horse: Scorch

Colour:
Bright chestnut with a white blaze

Height:
14.2hh

Personality:
Lively, mean, impatient

Pony Breed:
Show Pony x Thoroughbred

Elemental appearance:
Red eyes, mane and tail of dark
flickering flames

Elemental abilities:
Fire Horse - although not as
powerful as Ember, Scorch can heat
things up and cause small fires

Moonlight Riders

Meet all the True Riders of Moonlight
Stables and their amazing elemental horses!

Moonlight Riders

Fire Horse
LINDA CHAPMAN

Moonlight Riders

Storm Stallion
LINDA CHAPMAN

Moonlight Riders

Petal Pony
LINDA CHAPMAN

Moonlight Riders

Sea Foal
LINDA CHAPMAN

Do you have what it takes to become a True Rider?